Wired
Wonder Woof

Books by Robert Elmer

ASTROKIDS

PROMISE OF ZION

ADVENTURES DOWN UNDER

THE YOUNG UNDERGROUND

ROBERT ELMER

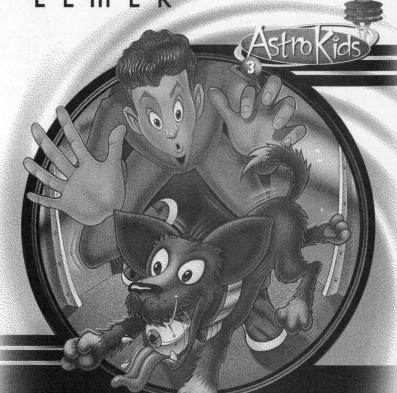

AstroKids

3

Wired Wonder Woof

BETHANY BACKYARD®

www.bethanyhouse.com

Published by Bethany House Publishers
A Ministry of Bethany Fellowship International
11400 Hampshire Avenue South
Bloomington, Minnesota 55438
www.bethanyhouse.com

Printed in the United States of America by
Bethany Press International, Bloomington, Minnesota 55438

Library of Congress Cataloging-in-Publication Data

Elmer, Robert.
    Wired wonder woof / by Robert Elmer.
        p. cm. — (AstroKids ; 3)
Summary: A smooth-talking Galaxian visitor to the space station shows unusual interest in the AstroKids' new space mutt, Zero-G.
    ISBN 0-7642-2358-5 (pbk.)
    [1. Space stations—Fiction. 2. Dogs—Fiction. 3. Christian life—Fiction.
4. Science fiction.] I. Title.
    PZ7.E4794 Wi 2001
    [Fic]—dc21

                                                                    2001001323

To Bill Myers,

a very funny guy.

Robert

Freckles

ROBERT ELMER is an Earth-based author who writes for life-forms all over the solar system. He was born the year after the first *Sputnik* satellite was launched, and grew up while Russia and the United States were racing to put a man on the moon. *Why not a boy on the moon?* he wanted to know. Today, Robert and his family live near a landing strip about ninety-three million miles from the sun, with their dog Freckles (who barks at incoming air traffic).

Contents

* * *

MEET THE
AstroKids

Lamar "Buzz" Bright

Show the way, Buzz! The leader of the AstroKids always has a great plan. He also loves Jupiter ice cream.

Daphne "DeeBee" Ortiz

DeeBee's the brains of the bunch—she can build or fix almost anything. But, suffering satellites, don't tell her she's a "GEEN-ius"!

Theodore "Tag" Ortiz

Yeah, DeeBee's little brother, Tag, always tags along. Count on him to say something silly at just the wrong time. He's in orbit.

Kumiko "Miko" Sato

Everybody likes Miko the stowaway. They just don't know how she got to be a karate master, or how she knows so much about space shuttles.

Vladimir "Mir" Chekhov

So his dad's the station commander and Mir usually gets his way? Give him a break! He's trying. And whatever he did, it was probably just a joke.

 1 Spy ✳ ✳ ✳

"WOOOOF!"

Alarms went off in my headset.

Waa-waa-waa-waa!

The huge wet thing kept coming at me. It was all I could see on my right, and on my left, and . . .

Phew! Dog breath!

I'd never been hit from all sides by 3-D slime-breath before. Have you?

Even worse, I felt myself spinning out of control when the big tongue sloshed me head on.

Up is down, down is up, spinning . . .

Whoa! Dizzy yet?

All this time, I was hearing a funny voice. It wasn't one of the other AstroKids who live on space station *CLEO*-7 with me. Not DeeBee or Buzz. Not Miko or Tag. This was a tinny voice, with an accent sort of like an English butler's.

"Oh, I do say," said the voice. "This is rather curious."

Who had found me? I couldn't tell. But *I* thought it was rather curious to be rolling across the rec-room floor, being chased by a slimy pink dog tongue.

"Quite a lively ball, isn't it?" asked the voice.

I jerked my head, trying to fly away. Too late.

"Shall we launch this one?" came the voice again.

A moment later, the dog looked down at me, its head turned to the side. By that time, I was upside-down, caught under a paw.

Of course, I was only *seeing* this. It wasn't really happening to me. It was all happening to my Remote-Float Eyeball Cam. I was just watching it through my viewer goggles.

QUESTION 01:

Hold it, hold it! Goggles? Remote-Float . . . Huh?

ANSWER 01:

We're talking about the Remote-Float Eyeball Cam. Belongs to my dad, but I kind of, well . . . borrow it sometimes. He uses it to keep track of repair work on the outside of *CLEO-7*. The Cam's about the size of a human eyeball, and it floats anywhere, indoors or out. Even back in the corner of a room, where nobody notices.

I was really sitting in my dad's lab on the other side of the station. (Not rolling on the floor in the *CLEO-7* rec room.) From there, I steered the Eyeball Cam with the goggles.

Remote control.

Piece of cake.

Yeah, I could see everything the Remote-Float Eyeball Cam saw: Move my head left, it looked left. Move my head right . . . you get the idea. Built-in sensors helped me smell and hear things, too.

Pretty cool, I'm thinking. No way the other AstroKids would ever see me. Not in a gazillion years.

One problem, though: I flew the Cam a little too low. You know, down to dog level.

No matter. I would still find out what I needed to know. No job is too hard for Mir Chekhov, Galactic Private Eye.

(By the way . . . please pronounce my Russian name properly. It's "MEER CHECK-off." Try it again. . . . There. That's better.)

Now, camera left. DeeBee was standing on her head in the middle of the rec room. She was watching *Star Bores*, episode 769, on a 3-D holo-screen. You know, *Baah-BAAH, bah-buh-buh-BAAH-baah . . .*

DeeBee's little brother, Tag, belched in time to the music.

"Have some manners, Tag," DeeBee said.

Tag listens to everything his big sister tells him. He uncorked another one, then asked, "When's that Galaxian pirate coming to the station?"

"Galaxian *Trader*," his sister corrected him. "Not a pirate. And he's supposed to arrive today."

"I still bet he's a pirate."

"How do you know, Mister Expert on Pirates?" DeeBee didn't sound as if she believed him. Of course, she never believed *me* about anything, either.

"You just have to see one." Tag rubbed his hands together. "Galaxians have big black beards and a parrot on their shoulder and a patch over one eye, and most of them have just one leg and a blaster pistol tucked into their belts, and . . ."

Camera right. Over in the corner, Miko and Buzz were playing a game of holo-chess. Miko didn't say anything. Nothing new there. She hasn't talked much since she came here as a stowaway on a transport shuttle.

And Buzz looked as if he was thinking. I suppose the leader of the AstroKids has to do a lot of thinking.

"Has anybody seen Mir lately?" Tag asked. "He hasn't been around for days."

Aha! I thought. *Now I'll hear what they really think about me.* Then I could figure out how to get them to like me—or at least how to make up for . . . well, I had quite a few things to make up for.

"He's been working for his dad a lot," said Buzz.

That was true.

Tag still looked worried about something. "But he doesn't know yet about M2—"

Ahh-OO-gahh! A warning buzzer sounded out in the hall. "Vessel landing in eleven point two minutes!"

The Galaxian? I wondered.

But I didn't wonder too long. Because here came the tongue again! I almost gagged. The dog was licking me—that is, the Eyeball Cam. And let me tell you, dog breath is not pretty, up close. What did Tag feed this pooch for breakfast, anyway? Dead mice?

"Whatcha got there, Zero-G?" asked DeeBee.

Whoops! I was caught. Now I was in trouble.

Big trouble.

2 Dog Breath ✳ ✳ ✳

Zero-G lifted his paw enough for me to start rolling again.

Nice doggy.

"It appears to be a ball, Mistress DeeBee," said . . . what? Zero-G, the dog? "And quite a lively one, at that."

I didn't see any dog lips moving. But now I was sure Zero-G was talking. He sounded just like an English butler trapped in a titanium can. (You know, "tie-TAY-nee-umm." Really strong metal.) Either that, or somebody was having fun with me.

I didn't want to stick around to find out. If I could just roll to the side, maybe I could slip away without being slimed again. But the slobber was slowing me down.

"Hey, I know what that is." Buzz spoke up from somewhere behind me. "That's a Remote-Float Eyeball Cam!"

Uh-oh.

"Which means," DeeBee said, "someone is spying on us!"

"A spy!" screeched Tag. "Cool!"

I tried to move the Cam, but no go. The slime glued me to the floor.

I confess I did feel a little guilty about the spying. But how else could I make up for my jokes that had crashed and burned . . . big time?

I'm not talking lame-o "knock-knock" jokes. These were much better. I had thought they were funny . . . at the time. You should have seen the looks on people's faces when they ate the Mercury hot sauce on their Jupiter ice cream.

Or when I set off all the station alarms. Heh-heh.

Making the station drones go wacko all over *CLEO-7* was a scream, too. Even if everyone else didn't think so.

But that was the problem. What did everybody else think? I had to find out what they thought was cool. Or funny. Or whatever. That way, I could be cool, or funny, or whatever, too.

Get it?

"Yeah, get it!" squeaked Tag. "Squish it! Stomp it! Launch it!"

Why not? Yes, let's see who can stomp on my dad's Remote-Float Eyeball Cam. It cost only about a million and a half.

I twirled my Eyeball Cam around—just in time to see four AstroKids about to pounce.

Yikes!

"Here, I will show you," Zero-G told them. "I take it in my mouth, after which you chase me around the station. Are you quite ready?"

Quite. They could chase Zero-G all over *CLEO*-7, through the blue labs, the repair center, the gardens, the apartments, the dining area, the control center. We'd go around in circles. After all, *CLEO*-7 is shaped like a deluxe lunar-burger. And thinking about lunar-burgers usually made me hungry.

But not this time. My only chance was to find the door, and fast.

Bam! I nearly lost my goggles as the Cam went flying. Someone must have kicked it.

"Whoops!" Tag twirled out of sight. "I didn't mean to—"

There was lots of reaching and grabbing and spinning. By that time, I was Dizzy with a capital *D*.

"Oomph!" Someone made a flying leap and

smothered the Cam. But I squeezed it out, then rocketed off a wall.

This reminded me of an old Russian game called "pinballski." People batted a little marble around a table, and it bounced from side to side, up and down, over and across. *Boinga-boinga.* Lights flashed, bells rang.

Just call me the Twenty-Second-Century Pinball. And I was about to lose my lunch.

For just a second, I saw an open door. My way out!

I aimed the Cam for a blinking red light in the hallway.

Ahh-OO-gahh! The alarm sounded again. "Vessel landing in seven point five minutes!"

For one wonderful moment, I thought I'd made it.

Until everything went dark.

"Gotcha!" said Buzz.

That's when I smelled it again. *Nyet,* nyet, nyet! Anything but dog slobber!

"Excellent job, Master Buzz," said the dog. "Now, lift your hand, and I take the ball. I run. You chase. Ready?"

"Wait a second, Zero-G," Buzz said.

This was going from bad to worse. From the grip of Buzz Bright's strong hand to the pink slime dungeon of

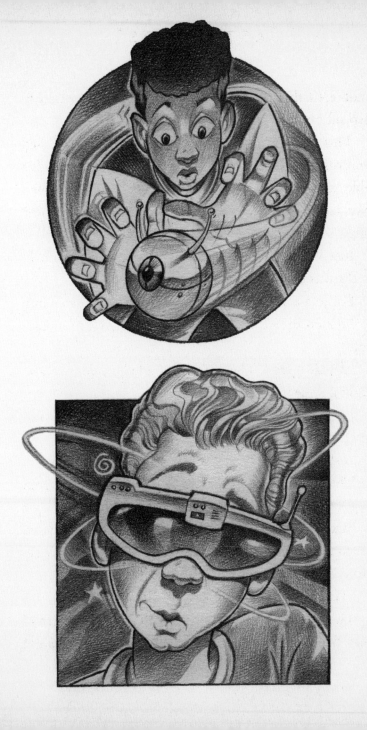

Zero-G's mouth. It was *dark* in there! And we were off, dog breath and I.

"Zero-G!" shouted the kids. "Let go!"

This was getting worser and worser, confusinger and confusinger. I held my stomach as we went bouncy, bouncy, bouncy down the hall.

"Now *this* is how the sport is played," the dog chuckled.

I still hadn't figured out two things:

01—How did this mixed-breed dog talk?
02—How did this mixed-breed dog talk with its mouth full of my father's super-expensive Remote-Float Eyeball Cam?

I didn't have the slobberiest idea. But I would find out.

3 Slimed

✳ ✳ ✳

"Ha-ha," Zero-G chuckled. This was a little pooch, so my Remote-Float Eyeball Cam was not far off the floor. A few centimeters, tops.

Anyway, Vunderdog and I raced down another hallway. In and out of legs and ankles. Up the hall, down the hall. Round and round and . . .

Dizzy yet? Me too.

Mostly it was dark. But I got little peeks through a couple of teeth once in a while. I heard the landing alarm again.

Ahh-OO-gahh!

I think we got in an elevator and whisked toward the hub. That's the middle of the station, where visiting spaceships land in our big space garages called shuttle hangars.

But by that time, I'd had it. I'd had all I could take of looking at the world through the mouth of a dog. So . . .

Hold it.

Stop.

Bag it.

And so on.

"No more!" I turned off the viewer function on my goggles and took a deep breath.

Ahh, back to real life. I'll look through my *own* eyes from here on, thank you. No more Eyeball Cam!

And now if I hurried, I might be able to find that crazy dog before everyone else did. But which way had he gone? To find out, I switched on the Heads-Up Find-It Beam. Then I listened.

QUESTION 02:

So how does this Heads-Up whatchamacallit work?

ANSWER 02:

Simple! The Heads-Up Find-It Beam is built into the goggles. A *moo* sound gets louder when you're close to the Remote-Float Eyeball Cam. That's how you know which way to go.

Anyway, I ran down hall BX-52, past a crowd of tekkies in their shiny blue coveralls. (Tekkies are the people who run all the technical stuff on this station. That's just about everything!)

Moo . . . went the Find-It sound.

The tekkies looked at me as if I had escaped from a pasture.

Moooo . . .

The homing sound grew still louder, the closer I got.

MOOOO!

This was it! I stopped outside the door to shuttle hangar 01. The door *svooshed* open, and I was sure: The Remote-Float Eyeball Cam was somewhere inside that big, empty shuttle garage. I just hoped it wasn't inside Zero-G's tummy.

I looked around at the high, round ceiling, the giant garage doors on both sides, the windows set into the side wall. The other AstroKids weren't there yet. They didn't have a Find-It beam to help them.

And there, in the corner, stood my four-legged thief.

Stood? Nyet, not quite. The hub is a weightless zone, so he floated a foot off the floor. Zero-G was a good name for him. (You know, Zero-*Gravity*.) He seemed to like being weightless.

"You!" I wasn't sure how to talk to the dog. Never talked to one before.

"Ha-ha." The dog wagged his tail and floated up as high as my shoulders. His hind end twisted in the air. I thought he was smiling, but that couldn't be.

Dogs can't smile. Can they?

"Sit," I told him. "Stay. Roll over."

"Roll over?" he asked. "So sorry, mate. I don't *do* roll over."

"But you're a dog." My gripper shoes kept me down on the hangar floor. "All dogs are supposed to do tricks."

"This dog does only one, my dear fellow: I run. You chase. Ready?"

"Nyet, I mean, no. I need my Remote-Float—I mean, my ball back." I stepped closer. Maybe I could grab the Eyeball Cam before he drifted away.

"*Your* ball? Oh no, dear fellow. It was I who found it."

"I know you did. But it's mine."

"You're a funny one. Perhaps we could go to the garden rooms, bark at some birds, roll in some dirt. What do you say?"

"Thanks, anyway," I told him. Now I could tell that the sounds were coming from a little black box on his collar. Weird.

"You're quite sure you won't come?" The dog

turned his head toward me. "You'll feel much better after a jolly roll in the mud. I always do."

This was silly. I grabbed for the Eyeball Cam, but of course Zero-G wasn't letting go.

"I say!" he yelled. "That's rather unfair. You're taking my ball!"

"It's not a ball, you silly mutt! You don't understand—"

"What doesn't he understand?" asked a girl.

Uh-oh!

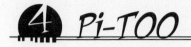 4 Pi-TOO　　　　＊ ＊ ＊

Whoops.

I turned to see the rest of the AstroKids busting into the shuttle bay. DeeBee Ortiz stood there with her hands on her hips and a frown on her face.

"It's not what it looks like," I started to tell her. Well, I guess it looked as if I was trying to take candy from a baby. I let go of the Eyeball Cam.

"Go ahead, doggie. Have your ball."

"Thanks, my good man," the pooch said. "Now I'll spit it out so you can throw it for me. I say, what fun!"

"Wait!" I reached again as Zero-G shook his head. Too late. He let go with a mighty *pi-TOO.*

The Eyeball Cam hit my ear with a splat, then hung there, dripping on me. (Remember, stuff floats when there's no gravity.) I picked it out of the air with two fingers. Yuk.

The Cam had been seriously slimed. It would need some deep cleaning.

"How did Zero-G learn how to talk?" I tried to change the subject.

"M2V," said DeeBee.

Like I was supposed to know what that meant.

"Mind to Voice," she explained. "It's an old idea, but no one has ever done it quite right."

"And you have?"

"She's a GEE—" Tag began, but his sister cut him off.

"Yeah, well, Zero-G thinks a doggie thought. The collar picks it up. Then a nano-computer turns that into words. And since I stored two hundred thousand words in the collar, he can say just about anything."

Pretty cool, I had to admit. And that English butler voice was classy.

"We were going to show you," added Tag, "only you've been so busy."

Probably true. But still . . .

"DeeBee just invented it," he went on. "We got the parts from our great-grandfather's junk box. Tiny speakers and everything."

"Same stuff you made your drone out of?" I pointed at the watermelon-sized silver drone floating next to DeeBee.

"Yeah!" Tag liked to talk. "Hey, MAC, wake up!"

QUESTION 03:

Quick, what's a MAC? Some neat kind of computer that's easy to use?

ANSWER 03:

Not exactly. But there's no time to tell you now. Keep reading. He'll tell you himself in just a second.

"Wait a minute. . . ." DeeBee put up her hand for him to be quiet and squinted in my direction.

Time for me to leave. I quickly wiped the slobber off the Eyeball Cam and slipped it into my pocket. Then I remembered what was still parked on my forehead—the viewer goggles!

"Wait a minute. It was *you*!" She pointed at me. "You're the one who was spying on us. How *rude*."

Busted. So much for Mir Chekhov, Galactic Private Eye.

"Oh, *these*?" I tried to look cool as I pulled the goggles off my forehead. "Maybe they're not what you think."

"Or maybe they are," said DeeBee.

"What *are* they for, then?" Buzz wanted to know.

"Uh, I was checking on some, uh, X-wave dishes on

the outside of the station."

"When?" asked Buzz. "Just now?"

"Uh, yesterday."

Which was true.

"So what about a few minutes ago?" asked DeeBee. "Why were you spying on us in the rec room?"

"Oh, that. Uh . . ." How could I explain without sounding totally lame?

DeeBee crossed her arms. She was not smiling.

"So you *spied* on us?" she asked. "That's really tacky, Mir."

"Oh, come on." I tried to calm her down. "Don't get all bent out of shape. Believe me, it was just—"

"*Believe* you?" DeeBee didn't. "How can we believe you about anything? You never 'fess up. You always try to make excuses. Like now."

Ouch.

"I'm sorry," I tried. "But . . ."

But what? That's when a red light started flashing up on the wall. And believe me, the timing was perfect. Couldn't have been better.

"Emergency landing in two minutes!" a voice echoed through the huge room. "Clear the shuttle bay!"

Emergency landing? Hey, no problem. I would have

been glad to clear out, except that Tag was holding on to my arm.

"Everybody to the view room," Buzz told us. "We'll talk about this later."

In the view room, we all piled around a holo-screen to see what was going on outside. Zero-G stood on his hind legs to peek out the view window, into the shuttle bay. We would be able to see the shuttle come in from there.

"What's happening, DeeBee?" Tag whispered to his big sister.

"See that?" She pointed to a 3-D holograph coming from a control panel. It showed a ship speeding straight toward *CLEO*-7. The ship had two huge wings, one on each side. They were turned sideways to catch solar wind. (You know, the sun's energy.)

"Here comes the Galaxian Trader," whispered Miko.

"I can't wait to see the pirate!" Tag whistled through his teeth.

"Tag," said DeeBee. "I told you—"

Suddenly the big outside doors started to rumble open. A few stars peeked at us from between the doors. A second later, the Galaxian's huge black ship came screaming into shuttle hangar 01.

ZHOOOOM! We could feel the buzz in our chests. Then a roar, and one of the big wings nicked the side door. A shower of sparks hit the floor.

5 Arrr!

The Galaxian stepped out of his ship in a *fisst*ing cloud of mist.

"How'd he land that big thing?" Buzz asked.

"That's a Galaxian?" I wondered aloud.

"Where's his beard?" asked Tag. He pressed his nose against the window to see better. "And what about the *gep gel*?" (That's *peg leg*. Tag is always doing that silly backward talk.)

I couldn't see any patch over the man's eye, either. No parrot on his shoulder. Not even a blaster pistol.

And no "Arrr, ye scurvy mates!"

In fact, he looked more like a vid-star than anything else. He wasn't that old, for one thing. Maybe in his twenties. He ran his hand over a nice crop of perfectly combed black hair. And after he checked his ship, he smoothed out the wrinkles in his nifty red-and-white satin flight suit.

No doubt about it: This guy looked one-hundred

percent cool. Even his gripper shoes had the latest svooshes on the sides. Nice touch.

His ship was even cooler. Imagine all black, polished to a sparkle, with silver windows in front and shiny chrome trim around the edges, too. And huge! It made our nicest *CLEO-7* shuttles look like toys. I cranked my head back to read the ship's name, painted in curvy silver letters on the side.

Lord Sliver's Revenge.

Huh? Hmm. Whatever. We hurried down the steps to the shuttle-hangar floor.

"Wow," said Tag. "Are you a Galaxian?" (Kind of the same way you would ask someone in a cape and a mask, "Wow. Are you Captain Universe?")

Our visitor's crooked smile was big enough to share with all five of us and still have plenty left over.

"Captain John Long Sliver, at your service." The grin didn't leave his face as he bowed. "Thrilled to meet you."

"No, you're not," chirped Zero-G.

Whoa! Nothing like a little word bomb. *Ka-BOOM!*

"Pardon me?" The Galaxian's eyebrows looked like humpbacked caterpillars caught in a Pluto ice storm. And his eyes pierced like black lasers. "Who said that?"

"I did." Zero-G poked his head between my feet.

"Because you're not thrilled at all. And do you know what else?"

"Zero-G!" gasped DeeBee.

I was thinking our lives were over. This talking dog was brave, fearless, or crazy. Maybe all three.

"Zero-G, I presume?" Captain Sliver turned to me. He must have thought *I* was talking.

And I was thinking, *This is not good.*

"It wasn't me." I backed away and held up my hands. "I'm Mir Chekhov, and my dad is the station commander, and—"

"Oh, really?" He looked impressed. "The station commander's son? Very good. Excellent."

Only it sounded more like "eksssss-ellent."

When I backed up, I bumped into MAC.

"Good morning." The drone picked a strange time to power up. "I am your Micro-Automated Companion, and I was created to serve you. Please press one if you want me to keep talking in English. *Para Español . . .*"

"Not now, MAC." DeeBee tapped a button on his side. "Uh, he still needs work."

"Danger, danger!"

MAC's three glowing yellow eyes twirled once on their stems, then pulled back with a slurping-the-bottom-of-the-milkshake sound. His claw hands went limp. But he still bobbed in the air, about waist high, humming.

"Pardon me, sir." Zero-G sniffed at our new guest. "But you are not as nice as you look."

Captain Sliver looked down at the floor and started to chuckle.

"My, my, what have we here?" The chuckle turned into a laugh. "Are *you* the one who was saying nasty things about me?"

"Look, but don't touch," grumbled the dog as Sliver bent down to pet him.

"Perfect," said the man. He was staring at Zero-G as if he had just discovered a long-lost stash of Jupiter ice cream. "I love little animals!"

"Yeah, for dinner," whispered Zero-G.

"What?" The Galaxian laughed. "I've never met a dog with a sense of humor."

"It's his collar," began DeeBee.

The captain nodded. "Ah yes. I've heard of M2V experiments, but I've never seen it work."

"He's a special dog," said Tag. "And DeeBee is a GEEN-ius."

"Yes, I can see. Say something else, my dog friend."

"Woof." Zero-G scratched his ear.

"Ha-ha. I like that. Hmm . . . you'd be perfect for . . ."

But he didn't finish.

Perfect for what?

"Er . . ." Mr. Sliver must have changed his mind. But he never stopped staring at Zero-G. "Who owns this beast—er, I mean, this fine animal?"

"I do," said Tag and DeeBee at the same time.

"We all do," added Buzz.

Miko nodded.

"No one owns me," said Zero-G. "I am my own."

"Of course you are," said the captain, and he air-washed his hands. "That will make things much easier."

Much easier?

He looked at me with a weird laser-beam gleam in his eye.

"We'll chat again soon, Master Chekhov," he told me.

"Sure." I shivered. "Sure thing."

Tour?
6 What Tour?

* * *

Please understand, I wasn't afraid of the Galaxian. Nyet, are you kidding? He seemed like a nice guy. Never mind all the dumb old space-pirate stories.

Shiver me timbers! They were just stories.

Besides, I really liked his cool ship. So the next day when he asked me if the AstroKids wanted a tour, how could I say no? I showed up right on time, after dinner.

Where's everybody else? I wondered. A step zipped me up to the main door. *Am I late?*

Zveef! Two shiny black doors slid to the side.

"Hello? Mr. Captain Sliver, sir? Buzz? DeeBee?"

A moving belt swept me inside. The door *zveefed* shut behind my back.

I'm not scared of the Galaxian, I'm not scared of the Galaxian, I'm not—

"Come in, come in!" he boomed.

I looked around at wall-to-wall controls and old lime-green control screens. Some of the controls flickered, like you'd get a shock if you brushed against them. And most were covered with greasy fingerprints. I ducked to keep from bumping my head.

Okay, so this was nothing like the ship's shiny outside.

Captain Sliver stepped around the corner with that permanent smile on his face. "Thank you so much for coming."

"Sure." I looked around again. "But is DeeBee here? Or Buzz?"

"Your friends? I'm sure they'll arrive in a moment."

"Maybe I'll wait outside until they do."

"No, please stay."

I stepped toward the door. It didn't open.

"Listen, my young friend," he purred. "I have a deal for you."

I gulped. "A deal? Uh . . . what about the tour?"

He laughed. "You'll like this better."

I turned around slowly, my back to the door.

"Allow me to get right to the point." He grinned. "I need the dog."

"Zero-G?" What did this stranger want with a space mutt? "Why?"

"For the Galaxian Super Show, of course. The *greatest* show in the universe!"

Oh, so *that's* why Captain Sliver had been so interested in Zero-G. He wanted him for an act. I'd heard of it. Who hadn't? "Is that the one with the fire-breathing space cats and—"

"And the dancing monkeys, yes, all that. But I'm always looking for new talent."

"Are they in your ship?" I pointed at a back room. That might be pretty cool to see.

"No!" He stepped in my way, then smiled again. "I mean, perhaps later. Right now, you have too many questions, my friend. I just want you to imagine your dog—"

"He's not *my* dog."

"Pretend for a moment." He waved his arm around the control room. "Your dog could be famous, beyond anything you could ever dream of. A star. Zero-G: The Wired Wonder Woof! He'd live a wonderful life, travel the Solar System, make lots of mo . . . mothers and little children happy."

"He would?"

"Of course." Captain Sliver's voice was smooth as a lava flow on Io. (That's one of Jupiter's moons.) "And you're the only one who can make it happen, Mir Chockoff."

"Chekhov."

"That's right."

"Why me?"

"Because none of your friends sees how *big* this is. But you see. You understand."

"How do you know?"

"Ha! I can tell from your face. Your clever mind shows through."

"Really?" I checked my reflection in a display. I looked green.

"Now, listen to me, my good man." He smiled. "I'm leaving three hours from now. I want that talking dog on board."

"I don't think he's for sale." I shook my head. "I can't just take him, can I?"

"No, no, no. You heard him yourself. He belongs to no one. But you're his friend. You will just invite him for a ride aboard the *Lord Sliver's Revenge*. Quietly."

"Uh, I don't know . . ."

"And if anyone asks what happened to the beast, you can tell them you saw the poor dog slip out into space through the shuttle-hangar doors. How sad."

"But that's not—"

"Tsk, tsk. Details. After that, I want you to show them what the kind Galaxian trader left you as a gift. A zipsuit? A space scooter?" He waved his hand at a holo-projector. *Zimm!* It lit up. "Take a look."

Take a look? He showed me 3-D pictures of some of the most awesome space scooters I'd ever seen. Two-seaters. Three-seaters. Hyper-drives. Very cool. Really expensive stuff, but . . . in trade for a dog? I think my mouth fell open.

"I see you like the idea." He grinned. "You could share your gift with your friends, of course."

"I, umm, already have a zipsuit." I swallowed hard.

"Then take the space scooter. Or perhaps something else."

I couldn't keep up with all the nifty things in his holo-catalog. *Anything* I wanted? No one's ever told me that before, even though the other AstroKids might think so. They think I'm spoiled, that my dad will buy me anything. That's not true. Not quite.

"Well?" Captain Sliver crossed his arms.

I heard the little voice in my head, whispering, *Don't do it!*

I shook my head.

"Listen, my young friend," he told me. "This is a chance of a lifetime."

"Sure, but I—"

"All you do is deliver me the animal. And his collar, of course."

"It's not going to be easy." I frowned but thought again of the shiny space scooter. It would be pretty cool. . . .

"Easier for you than for me, Mir. Although I *could* do this myself, you know."

With that, he guided me to the door.

"But remember!" He squeezed my shoulder. "This is just between you and me, eh?"

"Uh . . ."

"It's settled, then. I'll see you back here in two hours and fifty-seven minutes. I have to make a few more . . . deals. And then I take off."

Zveef! The doors just about caught me in the seat of the pants when I stepped out. And you know something?

Captain Sliver forgot all about the tour.

🚂 10-4   ✳ ✳ ✳

They say you can tell a lot about a person by the kind of friends that person has. Especially when the going gets tough.

I mean, "a friend loves you all the time," right? That's in the Bible. Proverbs, I think.

But a few minutes after my, uh, *tour* of the Galaxian's ship, you could tell how well I was doing in the friends department.

I was sitting in my dad's empty office. And I was having a man-to-man talk with a *drone.*

"You look nervous," said MAC. "Pulse 150, high blood pressure, sweaty palms, fast breathing . . ."

"You don't need to hold my hand, MAC."

"I am your Micro-Automated Companion. I am here to help you."

"Thanks, but *me?*"

"Yes, you. You are Mir Chekhov, are you not? Son of Station Commander and Mrs. Chekhov of *CLEO-7?*"

"That's me, but—"

"You live in cubicle 149-b."

"Everybody knows that."

"You have been a Christian since 2171."

"Right."

"Your favorite food is Jupiter ice cream, and you are always hungry."

My stomach rumbled.

"You say things before you think."

"That's not true."

"You want people to like you better, so you play jokes on them."

"Well . . ."

"And your underwear size is—"

"Okay, okay," I waved at MAC to stop. "I get the point. But listen, if you want to help, you should know that something really *stinks* on Captain Sliver's ship."

MAC clicked and turned circles. He did that when he was trying to think.

"I am sorry," he finally told me. "DeeBee has not programmed my olfactory program yet."

"Which means?"

"I cannot smell."

"No, no, I mean something's *wrong* on Captain Sliver's ship."

I explained what the Galaxian had told me.

"Why did you not say so before?" MAC waved his arms. "My scans show you are in very big trouble."

"Trouble is right." I sighed. "And Captain Sliver doesn't take 'no' for an answer, if you know what I mean."

"You do not mean—"

"Relax. I'm not going to give him Zero-G. We just need a plan."

"A plan? Mir, you need help! Do you pray?"

"Sure, I do."

"And have you told your father about all this?" MAC twirled and bobbed.

"Not yet." I scratched my head. "I need more proof."

"Then what about telling the other AstroKids?"

"They'll just think it's another one of my jokes."

"Some joke. But you have not even tried."

"Well, DeeBee for sure won't believe me. She never believes me."

"Then she should have been there."

"You mean for a tour of *Lord Sliver's Revenge*? Yeah." Now the lights in *my* head were finally coming on. I snapped my finger. "That's perfect, MAC."

I wasn't sure if our idea would work. But I had a feeling.

"Perfect?"

"Yeah," I told him. "There's *something* on that ship he doesn't want us to see. And I know exactly what to do. . . ."

* * *

Five minutes later, I had the good old Remote-Float Eyeball Cam de-slobbered, fired up, and flying again. MAC was floating beside me in Dad's lab. He was linked to the goggles so he could see the same thing I saw. We just needed to steer the Cam down a few hallways and into shuttle hangar 01.

Remote control.

Piece of cake.

Here we go, goggle-view!

"Slide the Eyeball Cam in behind this tekky," MAC told me. "Follow her. She is turning left into shuttle hangar 01."

"Right."

"No, Mir. Left."

"Left. Right."

"Say '10-4' so we do not get confused."

"Okay. I'm going 10-4 into the shuttle hangar."

I felt a tug as I tried to slip the camera in behind the tekky. We svooshed through the doors.

"Who let the dog out?" She waved at a couple of other workers and pointed to her feet.

What dog?

"Say, there, Ms. Technician," said a voice from the shuttle-hangar floor. "Would you care for a game of tug-of-war? A growling contest?"

Zero-G! What was he doing there? I watched through my Eyeball Cam. The dog wove the end of a long, stretchy cargo sling around the tekky's feet.

"Or perhaps I could tangle your feet up in knots. In and out, over and through . . ."

QUESTION 04:

What's a cargo sling?

ANSWER 04:

A cargo sling is like a giant slingshot. I mean GIANT, and with a very stretchy rubber band as thick as your finger. Hook up the cargo, pull it back, and *ZWING!* There it goes. It's for sending small cargo to places like the moon, without shuttles.

You say that doesn't sound real high-tech?

Maybe not. But hey, it works.

"Perhaps you'd rather play catch?" asked Zero-G. "I'll be glad to personally slobber on the ball for you."

"Sorry, pal." The tekky held up her hands. "I don't have anything to throw."

"Oh, but you do." Zero-G hopped up on his hind legs. "Look right behind you."

Ay! Not good!

"Oh?" She turned, but I was too quick. I zipped the Cam up behind her head to hide.

"Hmm." She looked around again, probably wondering what Zero-G was talking about.

I stayed behind her.

"Ball!" Zero-G called after us. "Come back here!"

Thanks a lot, Zero-G.

MAC and I were away from there as fast as I could point the Eyeball Cam toward the black Galaxian ship.

"Ball! Come back!"

Boinnggg! We hit the force field pretty hard. The field covered the Galaxian's ship like a pink see-through blanket.

"Lean into it," MAC told me. "I'll try to shut it off."

"10-4." So I leaned forward, putting all my Eyeball

Cam's power into getting through.

Spackle-CRAAZT . . . I heard the force field crackling in my ears. I saw gold sparkles, like you see when you stand up too fast. And finally . . .

Worse Than
8 Dog Breath ✳ ✳

BLOOP!

"We're through!" The Eyeball Cam slipped through the force field like a watermelon seed squeezed between two fingers. Dad's Eyeball Cam was made for stuff like this.

So here's what we'd do: Get in. Get pictures. And get out. We'd show the rest of the AstroKids what I'd seen, and more!

And then . . . well, one thing at a time. *Lord Sliver's Revenge* looked huge in my goggles.

Here we go, I thought. My hands shook as I zipped toward an open panel, under the main outside door. I was trying not to think what would happen if we got caught.

"Down a little more, then up . . ." MAC knew the way into this ship. I think he was programmed to know his way around every space vessel in the system.

"Are you sure it's this way?"

✳
59 ✳

"I am sure."

"All right." I held my breath. "Here we go."

I pointed the Cam into a slim tunnel full of wires and lights. I pushed forward.

So far, so good. But it felt kind of like a space walk on the cold side of the moon without a heated suit.

"Are you all right, Mir? You are shivering."

"I'm tiddly-riffic."

"Well, then, can you tell me where otters come from?"

"Otters? What. . . ?"

"From otter space!"

"Ohh," I groaned. "Please, MAC, not now."

"I was just trying to make you feel better at a nervous moment."

Thanks anyway. At least I was inside, getting closer to the main room. I could just make out a dim red glow up ahead, and . . .

"Gross," I whispered. "Do you smell that, MAC?"

Oh, right. I forgot.

"Well, be glad you can't," I told him. "It's worse than dog breath."

"Shh." MAC cut me off. "Listen."

"Owww!" It sounded like crying, only worse. Moaning. Groaning. Whatever was making the sounds really hurt. And believe me, it hurt just to listen.

"Ohhh" came another moan. Was someone in trouble? I was almost afraid to find out, but I hurried the Eyeball Cam along through the narrow tunnel. I ducked and dodged past wire bundles. The red light was just ahead.

"Yip! Yip! Yaooooh!" For just a second, it sounded like a wolf. But that couldn't be.

Or could it? About sixty seconds later, I found out. And I *couldn't* believe it. My Remote-Float Eyeball Cam had taken us inside a . . . prison.

You sure you want to know more? I still shake when I remember. The red glow made everything in the big room look kind of spooky. Boxes and crates were stacked everywhere. What a mess!

But that wasn't the bad part.

I scanned up a wall that was covered with tiny, dirty cages. Inside one, I saw a two-headed rabbit. And he couldn't get out because of the red force field stretched across the opening. Just like all the others.

QUESTION 05:
   Another force field?

ANSWER 05:

You've seen them in sci-fi shows. This was the real thing, though. These little force fields were like curtains of red electricity that kept the animals inside without bars. Get too close and . . . *zaaap!*

Anyway, the poor bunny was so crammed in his cage, his four long ears sparked right up against the force field. *Zaaap! Yip!*

Just above him, a triple-sized hummingbird scrunched into an even smaller space. He tried to flap his wings, but couldn't. There wasn't enough room. And his long beak . . . *zaaap!* He jerked back and bumped his head.

That had to hurt.

I counted at least a hundred cages, all of them filled with scared, weird animals. Freaks, I suppose, but they couldn't help it. Some of them were way too small, others way too big. Very strange.

In one, I saw a pocket-sized penguin curled up in a corner of a grimy box. In another, two zebra ponies who would have fit into your backpack. And in yet another, I spied a cute, furry thing that looked like a cross between a hamster and a green caterpillar.

A giraffe the size of a cat looked straight at my Eyeball Cam and cried.

"Not exactly Noah's ark," I told MAC.

I mean, nothing against cages. Lots of animals spend happy lives in cages. But this was different. Way different. It was dirty. It was cruel. It was . . .

The bunny whimpered again. Now I knew why Captain Sliver didn't want to give me a tour. And now I knew what I had to show everyone else.

My face turned hot, and I gritted my teeth. How long would it take me to break into this filthy slave ship and rescue them all?

"I believe these are the missing test animals from Moon Colony 3, Master Mir."

"What?"

"An experiment. Scientists wanted to see if they could raise animals without gravity."

"These animals?"

"I believe so."

"So why are they in Captain Sliver's ship?"

"I don't know. But you can see how it went wrong. The tests on the moon stopped when the animals disappeared."

I whistled. "So this isn't just a Galaxian Super

Show. This is a *stolen* Galaxian Super Show. With freak animals."

"I'm afraid so, Master Mir."

"Well, then, this is double-wrong. And we're going to stop it."

I just hoped it wasn't too late.

"Come on," I said. "We don't have much time!"

Believe Me!
9 Please?

✳ ✳ ✳

Two questions:

01—What if Captain Sliver was doing his own search for Zero-G?

02—And what if he found him?

I was afraid to find out. We used the Eyeball Cam to look for Zero-G in the shuttle hangars.

"He's not here!" MAC told me. So where else would the captain look? How about where the Astro-Kids usually hang out?

"We need to get to the rec room," I said. "Fast."

I tore off the Remote-Float Eyeball Cam control goggles and tossed them on my dad's workbench.

No more goggle-view!

But I wished I could whoosh through the station as fast as the Eyeball Cam. The best I could do was take a shortcut through a supply tunnel, a crawl space.

"Wait, Mir!" MAC's alarm went off behind me. "Danger! Danger! This isn't the best way."

Ka-BOING! I heard a huge crunch and a clang right behind me.

"Ouch!" MAC must have hit a metal floor beam. His alarm went off again.

"Come on, MAC. I know the way." We crawled along through the dark tunnel . . . farther . . . farther . . . left . . . right . . . and then . . . yes! I popped off a floor panel and squeezed up through a little opening . . . right into the middle of the rec room.

"Whoa!" DeeBee backed up a couple of steps. She saw my head pop up through the floor.

"Well, if it isn't the official *CLEO-7* spy!" Buzz was just walking in. "How's it going?"

"I can't talk now! Where's Zero-G?"

"You're funny!" Tag started to giggle. "You pop through the floor to ask us where the dog is? Why didn't you just call us on your wrist interface and ask?"

"Maybe I should have," I huffed. "But I wanted to make sure you would believe me."

"Believe you about what?" DeeBee crossed her arms.

"I'll tell you in a minute." I looked around the room. "But where's Zero-G?"

Buzz looked at DeeBee, DeeBee looked at Miko, and Miko looked at Tag.

Tag shrugged. "Zero-G? He was here a minute ago. I thought he was with MAC."

"He's not!" I told them. "MAC is with me . . . or he was, just a minute ago." The drone was nowhere in sight. "Look, this is important. Life and death important."

"Is this another one of your jokes?" DeeBee asked.

"WE HAVE TO FIND ZERO-G!" I hollered.

Well, that got their attention. And everybody in the rec room turned when we heard a door *svoosh* open.

"Somebody mention my name?" Zero-G poked his head in the door.

"There he is!" I probably didn't need to raise my voice.

Zero-G hopped up on Tag's lap. "Say, would anyone like to eat themselves sick, then stroll around the station looking for stray cats to chase? I believe there are a lot of jolly good sniffs out there."

"Look, there's no time for sniffing." I thought about locking the door so he couldn't get out again. "I've got something to tell you."

"All right, Mir." Buzz smiled, like he was waiting for the joke. "What is it this time?"

I took a deep breath and told them everything I knew. Well, just about everything. I didn't tell them how close I'd come to trading Zero-G for a space scooter. Everything else, though. I told them about the inside of the Galaxian's ship. And about the animals.

"Ha-ha, ha-ha . . ." Buzz was rolling on the floor. "How big did you say that giraffe was, Mir?"

I told him again. But that only made Miko and DeeBee laugh, too.

Tag was the worst of all. "You are so *ynnuf*, Mir." Tag took a deep breath, then broke up laughing again. "*So* funny."

"But I'm not *trying* to be funny," I told them. "I'm trying to tell you what I saw!"

"No way!" DeeBee shook her head.

"Way!"

"But you didn't see it with your own eyes, right?" DeeBee was doing her space-lawyer thing again. Great. Just great.

"No, but—"

"You say you saw it through the Eyeball Cam, right?"

"Well yes, but—"

"Aha!" DeeBee was moving in for the kill. "You can never be sure how big things really are when you see them through the Eyeball Cam, can you?"

"Maybe." I wasn't going to let her win this time.

"But I tell you, there were penguins and—"

"Penguins, too!" Buzz whooped. "That's rich! Penguins in space! Mir, you really do tell a good joke."

"Look. I can prove it!" I almost had to yell to make them hear me over all the laughing.

"How?" DeeBee wanted to know. The others stopped giggling long enough to listen, too.

"Okay. I know you think Captain Sliver's cool on the outside," I told them. "We all did. But MAC can show you what he's *really* like. He saw it, too."

By then, MAC had floated into the room, looking kind of crooked. He straightened out his floppy arms and floated up higher.

"Are you all right, MAC?" asked DeeBee.

"I think he bumped his, ah, head," I told them. "But, MAC, tell them what's inside Captain Sliver's ship."

"Oh, it's quite . . ." MAC started to explain. "It's quite . . . I mean, oh dear . . ."

"Tell them what you saw, MAC! Tell them what *we* saw."

10 Sit! Stay! Help! * * *

MAC's lights were flashing, all right. But I wondered if anybody was home. Maybe he had hit his head a little harder than I thought. A light twinkle-twankled on MAC's side, right above where he had been patched together with gray duct tape. Sometimes he reminded me of a used sonic cleaner unit.

"Good morning. I am your Micro-Automated Companion. I am here to help you."

"MAC," I groaned. "It's not morning anymore."

Big pause.

"Oh dear," he buzzed. "It is not?"

"It's three in the afternoon."

Another pause. I heard a grinding noise, like loose marbles.

Kind of like, *drumble, grackle, click, bzort.*

Not good. After all the *drumbling* and *bzorting*, he finally spoke up again.

"Well, I have good news and bad news for you."

"The bad news?" I didn't want to know.

"The bad news," bubbled MAC, "is that I seem to have lost my bubble memory circuits from the past sixty-two minutes, forty-five seconds. I know who you are, and I know who I am. But I'm afraid I can't remember the last hour."

Groan. He couldn't tell the other AstroKids what we saw!

"And the good news?" Okay. I might as well find out.

"The good news is that I will take only three minutes and forty-nine seconds to restart."

"Let me know if you have any more good stories to tell, Mir." Buzz shrugged and started for the door. "I've got to go do my chores. My dad wants me to reprogram the enviro-systems."

"I have to go, too." DeeBee followed him out while MAC bubbled quietly in the corner. Miko and Tag left, too, so it was just me.

"Nobody believes me," I mumbled. I threw a pillow across the room.

Zero-G ran after it and dropped it back at my feet.

"I do," he said. "I believe you."

Zero-G? After what I'd almost done to him?

I looked away. He was just a stray dog, after all. It

would have been so easy to give him to the Galaxian. End of story.

"Don't you remember who I am?" I asked him. "The spy who took your ball?"

But Zero-G only tilted his head to the side, perked his ears, and looked up at me.

"Dogs don't fuss about such things, old chap. We would rather chase our tails. Or chew things. I say, you wouldn't have something for me to chew, would you? Your gripper shoe, perhaps? I could shred it for you, if you like."

"Sorry. I have to go do something."

"Then I'll go with you."

"To the Galaxian ship? Are you kidding? That's just what he wants."

"But you said the animals need our help."

"I know. MAC will come with me. Are you recharged yet, MAC?"

MAC unfolded his arms with a pleasant *bee-boop* sound.

"Good morning. I am your Micro-Automated Companion. I am here to help you."

"Good. Then you're coming with me. Do you know how to shut down force fields?"

"Oh dear. My sensors tell me this is going to be dangerous."

I turned to Zero-G.

"And you're going to wait here."

"I don't *do* wait."

"You do this time. And lock the door."

I didn't wait for Zero-G to argue anymore. MAC and I headed for the Galaxian ship in a hurry. We were there in seven minutes, thirty-seven seconds flat.

"So, Mir, tell me something," said MAC. We pulled ourselves under the belly of the Galaxian's big black space freighter, looking for a way in.

"Tell you what?" I whispered back. I was still breathing hard from running.

"How does a dog on the moon get his hair cut?"

"Huh?"

"Eclipse it!" MAC chuckled and snorted.

I double groaned. Oh brother.

"Of all the drones in the universe, ours tells corny jokes! Why couldn't the bump on your head make you forget them, too?"

"Sorry, I was just trying to lighten things up."

"We don't need lightening up. All we need right now is to get in through that door. See what I mean?"

I pointed to a small square hatch in the belly of the

ship. "Can you open it for us, MAC? Looks like an electron combo-lock."

"Ha!" The floating drone chuckled. "You are thinking of the old *Star Bores* movies, where that little wastebasket on wheels opens doors. I am not like that."

"Fine. Here." I reached up to tap the door, and . . . uh-oh! Remember the force field? My fingertip went *bzzt* and bounced back at me. Ouch! Don't try this at home.

"No go." MAC told me what I had already learned the hard way. "We cannot get in this way, unless someone turns off the force field from inside."

Now what? We were running out of time. I sat down on an old cargo sling to think.

Okay, less than . . . I looked at the numbers on my wrist interface. Less than two hours until Captain Sliver would take off.

A 3-D face popped up above my wrist as I was looking.

Buzz! But he was kind of fuzzy, only half there. No nose or ears.

"Have you seen Zero-G?" he asked. His nose came back. "He *never* misses dinner."

For a second I thought the worst. Zero-G, missing?

"No, I haven't seen him."

"Hmm." Buzz squinted. "Well, then, where are *you*? I wanted to tell you I was sorry for laughing at you. It's just that you're so funny sometimes."

"It's okay. But listen, Buzz—"

"Can you speak up? I can hardly hear you."

"We're hiding under the pirate's ship," I whispered.

"A pie rat? What's that?"

"No, the *pirate*. Captain Sliver's ship. We're hiding, and—"

"Heidi? Heidi who?"

"No." I sighed. "I *said*—"

But that's all I said. I snapped off my interface when we heard the *zip-zip* sound of gripper shoes coming closer.

Captain Sliver?

Good Chance 4
Major Trouble

✳ ✳ ✳

"I want all those fuel pellets loaded in there right away!" boomed a man's voice. He did not sound happy.

"Yes, sir, Mister Captain Sliver, sir."

I looked at MAC and held a finger to my lips. No jokes now! A pair of fancy svoosh sneakers walked by. Captain Sliver's. They stopped a few meters away.

By that time, we could hear him plain as an ion storm.

"Computer!" barked the man. "Let me in."

"Identify, please," came a sweet, mechanical voice.

"Sliver, Captain John Long. One, six, alpha, two, nine."

The computer thought about that for a moment.

"Force field is down," it finally told him. "But you don't have to be grouchy about it. You may now enter."

"Arrr . . ."

A moment later, he disappeared up the steps into

his ship. But, hot dog! This was our chance, too. I reached up and touched a little lighted button on the panel above our heads.

Yes! It svooshed open. I grinned at the drone. A dim red light washed down on us.

"Are you impressed yet?" I whispered.

"I could not have done better myself," said MAC. "But are you sure this is safe?"

"Sure, it's safe." I hoped he didn't see my hands shaking. "Safe as, uh . . ."

I looked up at the big black monster we were crawling into. Safe as what? Safe as hitchhiking on a comet? Safe as a vacation to the sun?

"Warning! Warning!" MAC started swinging his arms. "My scanners show high danger and a very good chance of getting into major trouble."

"Shhh!" I batted his arm away. "Just follow me. And keep your three eyes open for Captain Sliver."

This was not the same as sending the Remote-Float Eyeball Cam inside for a peek. Same place, sure. But this was *us*, the real deal, crawling into a creepy room full of creepy little cages in a creepy black shuttle. I took a deep breath and nearly gagged.

Oh yeah. Creepy smell, too.

"Here goes." I reached up and pulled myself through the opening.

"Wait for me!" MAC hung on to my shirt.

And then we were inside. A kid with a drone wrapped around him. I got up off my knees and blinked in the dim red light.

"So this is the place." MAC wouldn't let go. It was the same room we had scoped out with the Eyeball Cam.

"Oh, wow!" I could hardly believe it, now that I was seeing things for myself. The cages, the red light from the force fields, everything.

I noticed two tiny chimpanzees crammed into a cage. They stared at us from behind the force-field curtain, holding on to each other. They looked like a mom and her baby, or maybe a big sister and little brother. I reached out my hand, but the force field kept me out.

"Hey, fella."

"EEE!" They both pushed back as far as they could.

Whoa, I thought. *Talk about scared.*

But I didn't blame them. I'd be scared, too.

"I believe the force field controls are over here," said MAC. "Do you still need me to open the cages?"

"Sure, I do." I peeled the drone off my shirt. "Now, let's—"

I froze at a sound right below us.

"Did you hear that?" I whispered.

MAC twisted his eyes to look back through the open floor hatch we had just crawled through.

"I say, gentlemen," came a little voice.

Uh-oh.

"A small animal," MAC announced. "Thirty-one centimeters long. Four legs. Canine species, I believe it is. . . ."

A head peeked up through the opening, then wrinkled its nose and disappeared.

"Zero-G."

"Zero-G!" I hissed.

"Greetings." A moment later, the dog popped back up to join us. "I say, chaps, I'm hungry. Is it launch-time, yet?"

Very funny. I parked my hands on my hips. "What are you doing here? I told you to stay."

"My dear boy, I don't *do* stay." Zero-G looked around and sniffed. "I don't do cage cleaning, either. HOO-boy!"

"You have to go back." I groaned and held my head. This was turning into a major astro-headache.

"Oh, no, no, no. I couldn't do that."

"Listen, Zero-G, I don't have time to stand here and

argue. Why don't you go back and fetch help?"

"Fetch help?" The dog could be as thickheaded as a meteor. "I *am* help."

I sighed and looked around at the room. Okay, I know I'm not perfect—ask the other AstroKids. But I know what's right and wrong. Hey, I read my Bible!

And I figured that what Captain Sliver was doing was just plain wrong. Never mind the dirty little cages with their zapping force fields. These animals were stolen!

Maybe we could do something about it—MAC, Zero-G, and I. Maybe we could shut down the force fields and set those animals free.

And then what?

Well, one thing at a time, right?

"Master Mir." MAC tapped on my shoulder with one of his arms.

"Not now," I whispered back. Maybe the palm switch on the wall by the door would cut off the force fields. I tried it.

Nothing.

"Master Mir!" MAC was getting louder.

And what was that? Zero-G, growling?

Weird.

Three things happened when I turned around:

01—The spit in my mouth turned dry.

02—My knees started knocking.

03—Captain John Long Sliver blocked the doorway, his
    arms crossed.

Vacation 12 to Pluto

✳ ✳ ✳

"What are you doing in here?" growled Captain Sliver.

Zero-G growled back.

I had to think of something fast. "You said to bring the dog," I told him. "Here he is!"

Which was true. But Captain Sliver wasn't buying it. I mean, like everyone else, he didn't believe me, either. I could tell.

"You didn't come in through the main door."

"Oh, you would have seen us if we had," chirped MAC. "And then we could not have freed all these poor animals."

Whoops. Drones aren't too good at keeping secrets.

"Heh-heh." I tried to grin, but my heart was beating at hyperspeed. "DeeBee said he needed a little work, remember? He says funny things sometimes. Tell him a joke, MAC."

"Yes, of course. Perhaps, er, what did the drone

have to do before she could wear earrings?"

"Tell him, MAC." I inched toward the escape hatch.

"She had to get her gears pierced! Hee-hee."

The Galaxian scowled while MAC kept it up.

"How can you tell if a planet is married?"

"Keep going," I whispered.

"It has a ring around it!"

"Belay that!" This time, the Galaxian sneered. What had happened to the big smile?

"Ah, ancient, seagoing pirate talk, I see." A couple of MAC's lights blinked extra fast. "You mean, be quiet."

"So, ah, feel free to use those jokes in your show, if you like." I edged toward the open door in the floor. "No charge. We were just leaving."

Just another step.

But the Galaxian waved his hand over a wall control panel. The trapdoor *zvooped* shut before I could get there.

"I don't think so." His voice was flat.

"Hey, wait a minute!" I found the words to speak up. "You can't keep us here!"

"Ah, but I can't just let you leave now." He pointed at the animal cages. "Not after what you've seen."

"Dead men tell no tales," droned MAC. "That is more pirate talk." MAC grabbed on to my shirt again.

"I don't care what you say." Now my cheeks were getting hot. "I'll just call my dad."

Or the AstroKids. Anybody! I reached for my wrist interface.

"Go ahead." Sliver grinned, but it wasn't friendly like before. "You'll find it doesn't work in here."

I pressed all the buttons on my wrist interface. *Click, click.* Nothing. I wished he weren't right.

"I told you he was trouble," added Zero-G. The hair on the back of his neck stood up. "Trouble with a capital *T.*"

"Ah," said Sliver, "but you can't always believe everything you see, can you, now."

That's for sure.

"Take me, for instance. Good-looking. Well dressed. Successful. Who would guess how humble I really am? And kind, too."

He bent down and tried to scratch Zero-G, but the dog pulled back his head and growled.

"And oh, how I *love* little animals," added Sliver.

"You said that before," whispered Zero-G.

"So I did." Captain Sliver stood up. "I'd love to stay and chat, but we must be on our way. Make yourselves comfortable. It's a long way to the outer system, me buckos."

This is when I would have made my move. Run. Scream. Attack. Do a karate kick, like Miko.

But I didn't have a chance. That scurvy space pirate just chuckled and backed out of the room. The door *zvooped* behind him.

"Come on back here, you . . ." I pounded on the door. *Thoink-thoink-thoink.*

Ouch. You didn't expect it to open, did you?

"Don't worry, matey." I could barely hear him. "If you behave, I'll let you off someplace pleasant. I hear Pluto is nice this time of year."

Yeah, nice—if you like four hundred degrees below zero.

"You can't do this!" I yelled.

He could, and he did. All we could do was watch him through the round window in the door.

Watch the
15 Hairdo!

* * *

Of course, my screaming and pounding didn't do any good. We could see the back of Captain Sliver's head at the controls. He pretended we weren't there and prepared for takeoff.

We could even see past him, through the front windows. The shuttle-hangar double doors opened to the stars. Three green lights blinked on. Go.

"No!" I yelled.

By that time, I could feel the rumble of our take-off thrusters.

"Launch time," said Zero-G.

"Whoa!" I grabbed for a handhold as the boosters kicked in and the ship began to move.

Some of the animals whimpered.

"Don't worry, Master Mir." Zero-G was trying to make me feel better. "We won't be gone long."

"How can you say that?" Maybe his little brain didn't get it. "You're going to be put in one of these cages, too. Don't you see? Part of Captain John Long Sliver's Space Freak Show. Me? I'm headed for a permanent vacation on Pluto. And MAC's probably going to end up a pile of spare parts."

"No, he's not."

"Oh, come on."

But suddenly something felt different.

I looked around. "Are we slowing down?"

"Slowing down and going home," said Zero-G.

I had no idea what he was talking about. And from the looks of it, neither did Captain Sliver. He was punching buttons as if his life depended on it. A big red light was blinking on his control panel.

Wah-wah-wah! A warning buzzer came on.

Wooo-wooo-wooo! There went another one.

"Do you know what's going on?" I asked Zero-G.

Even MAC looked at him.

"I told you, chaps." He sat down and scratched his left ear. "We're going home."

Then I felt it. Like an elevator rushing sideways. The animals in their cages slid to the other side.

"Ah, home." Zero-G kept scratching. "Where a dog can still have an evening's fun with a good plate of greasy leftovers."

I held on for balance.

Zero-G didn't seem to notice. "Home. Where I can always chase the cats on deck 43-G. You know—dogs rule, cats drool, that sort of thing."

I grabbed with both hands to hold on.

"Home. Where I can bark all night."

MAC waved his arms. "But we are now flying . . . backward!"

Whoa! We were.

A moment later, I tried to peel my nose off the door. Nothing doing.

"MAC, can you get off me?" I grunted. "Feelzh like yur control panel ish pokin zhe middle ov my back."

You would sound funny, too, if your lips were smooshed into the door.

"I am so sorry, Mir. But I cannot move."

"Ish okay." My cheek was smooshed, too. At least I had a good view of Captain Sliver.

Our villain of the day was strapped in, still punching buttons like a wild man. Probably trying to figure out what had turned his spaceship into a giant yo-yo. You know, the old toy on a string? I saw one in a museum once. Up and down. Down and up.

"Here we go again!" reported MAC.

How had this turned into a wild space carnival ride?

We flew into the shuttle-hangar front doors and out the back ones.

Then back again, frontward.

WHOOSH!

Then back again, backward.

HSOOHW! (That's "whoosh" spelled backward.)

Then back again, frontward.

WHOOSH!

Then . . . you get the idea.

We had now whooshed back and forth about ten times before I finally figured it out. "Somebody must have tied that huge cargo-sling rubber band in the shuttle hangar to the ship's landing gear," I sputtered. "And it wasn't me."

"Not I," said the drone.

We both looked at Zero-G.

"No way!" I gasped.

"Way," said the drone.

"In and out, over and through," said Zero-G.

"You?" I could hardly believe it.

So we weren't going anywhere after all. No long vacation on Pluto, thanks to Zero-G. Who would have thunk a little dog would be able to tie such strong knots?

He let me rub his furry head.

"Watch the hairdo," he said. But he was smiling, if dogs can smile.

So were all the other AstroKids when we finally made it back to the shuttle hangar in one piece. A couple of big-armed security guys took Captain John Long Sliver away. And actually, the kids were falling all over themselves, trying to tell me they were sorry.

Tell *me* they were sorry? *I* was the one who always made such a mess of things!

"We should have listened to you," DeeBee said.

"Yeah," agreed Buzz. "I guess Captain Sliver wasn't as cool as he looked on the outside, huh?"

Boy, that was for sure.

"Does this make up for my past bad jokes?" I asked.

"You're silly." Buzz took the lead as we left the shuttle hangar. "You don't have to *do* anything for people to like you. We like you, okay?"

Okay, okay. I started to smile.

"But one thing," DeeBee added. "From now on, we've got to stick together. No more spying and stuff."

I nodded. We left the hub just then, and gravity kicked in. My knees folded as I tried to walk down the hall. I was still shaky from the *whoosh-whoosh* ride.

"Hold on to my shoulder," Buzz said.

I told them maybe I just needed something to eat. A

chocolate Jupiter shake, maybe. But I did what Buzz told me.

"Take it easy," said Miko.

I took it easy. I took DeeBee's shoulder, too.

"It *was* pretty cool," chirped Tag, "watching the Galaxian's ship whoosh back and forth."

Yeah, with me in it. Cool? For the first time in a long time, I wasn't thinking about cool. Cool wasn't what something looked like on the outside, but what was going on inside.

"Which reminds me," said MAC. "Why was the AstroKid always hungry in space?"

"I don't know, MAC," I said, "but I have a feeling you're going to tell us."

"Because he lost his launch!"

Groan.

✳ ✳ ✳

If you're wondering what happened to the mini-animals, you should have seen the parade a few minutes later.

They followed Zero-G out of shuttle hangar 01, single file, while everybody on *CLEO-7* clapped and cheered. The pocket giraffe, the itty-bitty penguin, the teeny chimps . . . hundreds of little critters, all in a row.

Come to think of it, though, I never did see what happened to the fuzzy green caterpillar-hamster thing. Did anyone else remember seeing it inside the *Lord Sliver's Revenge*? I thought for a moment what would happen if any of the animals got lost in the station. Especially a creepy-crawly kind of animal.

But, oh well. The animals were okay, as far as we could tell. They were rescued and going back to where they belonged.

Thanks to the Wired Wonder Woof!

RealSpace Debrief

* * *

It's Launch Time
Three ... two ... one ... *BOOM!*
We Have Lift-Off!

Ever seen a shuttle launch from Cape Canaveral in Florida? Big rockets need a lot of blast-off power to escape the Earth. That's because gravity holds us to our planet. (Gravity is pretty strong stuff.)

The reason why spaceships are so large is to hold all the fuel they need to make that blast-off power. After all, there are no service stations in space.

At least, not yet.

But once we get into space—ah, here's where it gets interesting. No air means nothing to slow a spaceship down. Still, it's a long trip, even to our nearest neighbor in space. Think of it this way: If we were driving at freeway speeds twenty-four hours a day with no stopping, it would take six whole months to reach the moon. Want to drive to the nearest star? Better figure on having fifty million years to spare!

Space is a big place. (No surprise, considering the big God who made it!) If you want to get around, you'd better step on the gas. Or maybe hoist the sails.

What? Sails? That's right. Solar sails. Remember how Captain Sliver had them on his ship? Actually, we called them "wings" in our story, but they're the same thing. Well, people have been dreaming about "sailing" in space for years.

Seriously! All day, every day, the sun spits out tiny charged particles in every direction—at a million miles an hour! The trick is catching them. These energy bits are so tiny that it takes oodles to push anything. But the idea is that a huge aluminum-foil sail might catch enough of the sun's energy to sail a spaceship away from the sun.

It might take a while to get going with a solar sail. But once you're up to speed . . . *zip!* And the best part would be that you don't need to drag around a lot of fuel. Just like in a sailboat.

Of course, solar "wind" isn't wind, the way we know wind here on earth. But just like in a sailboat, you might be able to use it to zigzag in just about any direction you want to go.

You might wonder why we don't feel the solar wind here on earth. The globe's magnetic field makes a bubble of protection over us. That's the way God planned it, too.

Now, solar sails aren't the only way to get around in space. Another idea scientists like is called ion power. It's based on the same force that pushes two socks apart when you take them out of a hot dryer. Scientists have been working on this one even longer than solar wind.

Ion engines depend on electricity, magnets, and something called xenon gas. An ion engine shoots power out the back of a hollow tube at sixty thousand miles per hour. That can push a small spaceship.

No, ion power can't launch you from the surface of the earth. It's not *that* powerful. But once it gets going, an ion engine can run for months or even years.

Solar sails, ion engines, even giant slingshots. Sounds pretty far out, right? Maybe not. The first-ever ion engine is already pushing a real space probe called *Deep Space 1* through the solar system. Which only goes to show that science dreams are turning into science reality sooner than we might think!

Want to find out more about spaceships? Then check out:

- "Space and Astronomy for Kids" (on the Web at *www.liftoff.msfc.nasa.gov/realtime/JTrack*). Pretty good info for kids about rockets, shuttles, and satellites.
- Send Your Name to Mars (on the Web at *www.spacekids.hq.nasa.gov/2001*). Tells how to get your name on a CD that's really going to Mars!
- Johnson Space Center (on the Web at *www.jsc.nasa.gov/pao/students*). Cool kids' links to everything from shuttle info to the latest on the *International Space Station*.

And the Coded Message Is...

✳ ✳ ✳

You think this ASTROKIDS adventure is over? Not a chance. Uh-uh! No way. Negative. Nope. Because here's the plan: We'll give you the directions, you find the words. Write them all on a piece of paper. They form a secret message that has to do with *Wired Wonder Woof*. If you think you got it right, log on to *www.bethanyhouse.com* and follow the instructions there. You'll receive free ASTROKIDS wallpaper for your computer and a sneak peek at the next ASTRO-KIDS adventure. It's that simple!

WORD 1:
chapter 3, paragraph 2, word 17 _____

WORD 2:
chapter 5, paragraph 10, word 1 _____

WORD 3:
chapter 4, paragraph 3, word 5 _____

WORD 4:
chapter 1, paragraph 16, word 8 _____

WORD 5:
chapter 12, paragraph 3, word 12 _____

WORD 6:
chapter 12, paragraph 8, word 8 _____

WRiTE iT ALL HERE:

_____

_____

(Hint: Old Testament, in the book of 1 Samuel.)

Contact Us! ✳ ✳ ✳

If you have any questions for the author or would just like to say hi, feel free to contact him at Bethany House Publishers, 11400 Hampshire Avenue South, Minneapolis, MN 55438, United States of America, EARTH. Please include a stamped, self-addressed envelope if you'd like a reply. Or log on to Robert's intergalactic Web site at *www.coolreading.com.*

Launch Countdown

* * *

AstroKids 4:
Miko's Muzzy Mess

Mild-mannered Miko Sato thought she was the only stowaway on *CLEO*-7. So did the rest of the Astro-Kids—until they discover cute, furry animals hiding in the walls of the space station!

No problem, right? Sure, at first. But when Miko feeds them just a nibble of chocolate, things start to get out of hand. Before long, the station is crawling with thousands and thousands of hungry muzzies.

What a nightmare—and Miko thinks it's all her fault! How will the AstroKids ever get out of *this* mess?

Series for Young Readers*
From Bethany House Publishers

THE ADVENTURES OF CALLIE ANN
by Shannon Mason Leppard
Readers will giggle their way through the true-to-life escapades of Callie Ann Davies and her many North Carolina friends.

ASTROKIDS™
by Robert Elmer
Space scooters? Floating robots? Jupiter ice cream? Blast into the future for out-of-this-world, zero-gravity fun with the AstroKids on space station *CLEO-7*.

BACKPACK MYSTERIES
by Mary Carpenter Reid
This excitement-filled mystery series follows the mishaps and adventures of Steff and Paulie Larson as they strive to help often-eccentric relatives crack their toughest cases.

THE CUL-DE-SAC KIDS
by Beverly Lewis
Each story in this lighthearted series features the hilarious antics and predicaments of nine endearing boys and girls who live on Blossom Hill Lane.

JANETTE OKE'S ANIMAL FRIENDS
by Janette Oke
Endearing creatures from the farm, forest, and zoo discover their place in God's world through various struggles, mishaps, and adventures.

THREE COUSINS DETECTIVE CLUB®
by Elspeth Campbell Murphy
Famous detective cousins Timothy, Titus, and Sarah-Jane learn compelling Scripture-based truths while finding—and solving—intriguing mysteries.

*(ages 7–10)

Series for Middle Graders* From BHP

ADVENTURES DOWN UNDER · by Robert Elmer
When Patrick McWaid's father is unjustly sent to Australia as a prisoner in 1867, the rest of the family follows, uncovering action-packed mystery along the way.

ADVENTURES OF THE NORTHWOODS · by Lois Walfrid Johnson
Kate O'Connell and her stepbrother Anders encounter mystery and adventure in northwest Wisconsin near the turn of the century.

BLOODHOUNDS, INC. · by Bill Myers
Hilarious, hair-raising suspense follows brother-and-sister detectives Sean and Melissa Hunter in these madcap mysteries with a message.

GIRLS ONLY! · by Beverly Lewis
Four talented young athletes become fast friends as together they pursue their Olympic dreams.

MANDIE BOOKS · by Lois Gladys Leppard
With over five million sold, the turn-of-the-century adventures of Mandie and her many friends will keep readers eager for more.

PROMISE OF ZION · by Robert Elmer
Following WWII, thirteen-year-old Dov Zalinsky leaves for Palestine—the one place he may still find his parents—and meets the adventurous Emily Parkinson. Together they experience the dangers of life in the Holy Land.

THE RIVERBOAT ADVENTURES · by Lois Walfrid Johnson
Libby Norstad and her friend Caleb face the challenges and risks of working with the Underground Railroad during the mid–1800s.

TRAILBLAZER BOOKS · by Dave and Neta Jackson
Follow the exciting lives of real-life Christian heroes through the eyes of child characters as they share their faith with others around the world.

THE YOUNG UNDERGROUND · by Robert Elmer
Peter and Elise Andersen's plots to protect their friends and themselves from Nazi soldiers in World War II Denmark guarantee fast-paced action and suspenseful reads.

*(ages 8–13)